The Great Thanksgiving Food Fight

Michael G. Lewis
Illustrated by Stan Jaskiel

PELICAN PUBLISHING COMPANY
GRETNA 2017

*The word "Pelican" and the depiction of a pelican are
trademarks of Pelican Publishing Company, Inc.,
and are registered in the U.S. Patent and Trademark Office.*

ISBN: 9781455622856
E-book ISBN: 9781455622863

Printed in Korea
Published by Pelican Publishing Company, Inc.
1000 Burmaster Street, Gretna, Louisiana 70053

To my cherished friends, by whom I am truly blessed.
Thank you for all the times you've made me ponder life,
shed a good tear, or laugh so hard I thought I would die.
But what a way to go. —M. G. L.

For J Squared, the Pauses, KK and The Big D, Bernie, Chuck,
Jon, RICH, Bob U., Bob H., Brad, The Yonk, Diane, Kid
Kleeman, Uncle Al, The Big Cheese, aka Raoul Parcheesi,
Godfather Billy, A Dowse of Harriman, Gunta, Bueno Sera
Giovanni, and . . . The Old Man —S. J.

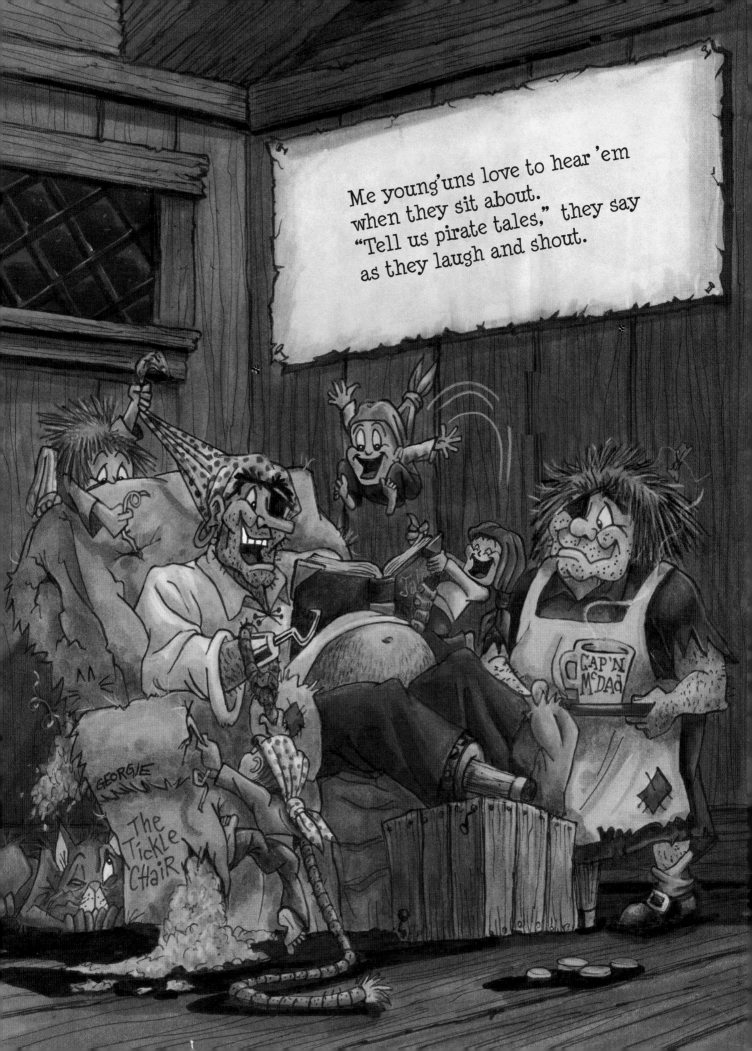

"Got a treasure chest of tales
that I'll share with you
of me younger days when I
sailed the ocean blue.

Steal we did on land and sea,
fillin' up the hold
of our ship the *Knotty List*
with silver and gold.

Now I had a hungry crew
turnin' quickly foul.
O'er the roar of wind and waves,
heard their stomachs growl.

"Ain't never seen so much food!"
was all that we could mutter.
Meats and pies of every kind,
even bread and butter!

We could smell that lovely food
from the *Knotty List,*
knowin' this was one grand feast
that could not be missed.

"We're a humble fishin' crew
down a bit on luck.
Thought we smelled fresh-baked bread
and some roasted duck."

Actin' all polite, we wuz,
asked if we could eat.
They led us to the tables,
offerin' us a seat.

'Twasn't long before they knew
somethin' wasn't right—
when we filled our pockets with
everythin' in sight!

Then I spied some pumpkin pie—
speared it with me hook!
They all turned and fixed on me
with a startled look.

"Pirates!"

screamed that pilgrim man.
"That's why they're so rude!
Here to ruin Thanksgiving Day
and steal all our food!"

I jumped up on the table,
gave a battle cry!
Then one of them pilgrim folk
hit me with a pie.

'Twas a full-on battle now
(arrr, a dreadful sight!)
known throughout the pirate world
as the Great Food Fight!

"Plunder all that you can steal,"
I screamed to me crew.
"I've taught you dregs all these years.
You know what to do!"

One fearless chief joined the fray,
grabbin' Dirty Davey.
Dragged him over to a bowl
and stuck his head in gravy!

A tug o' war broke out then
between Poutin' Pam
and a tough ol' pilgrim lass
o'er a boiled ham!

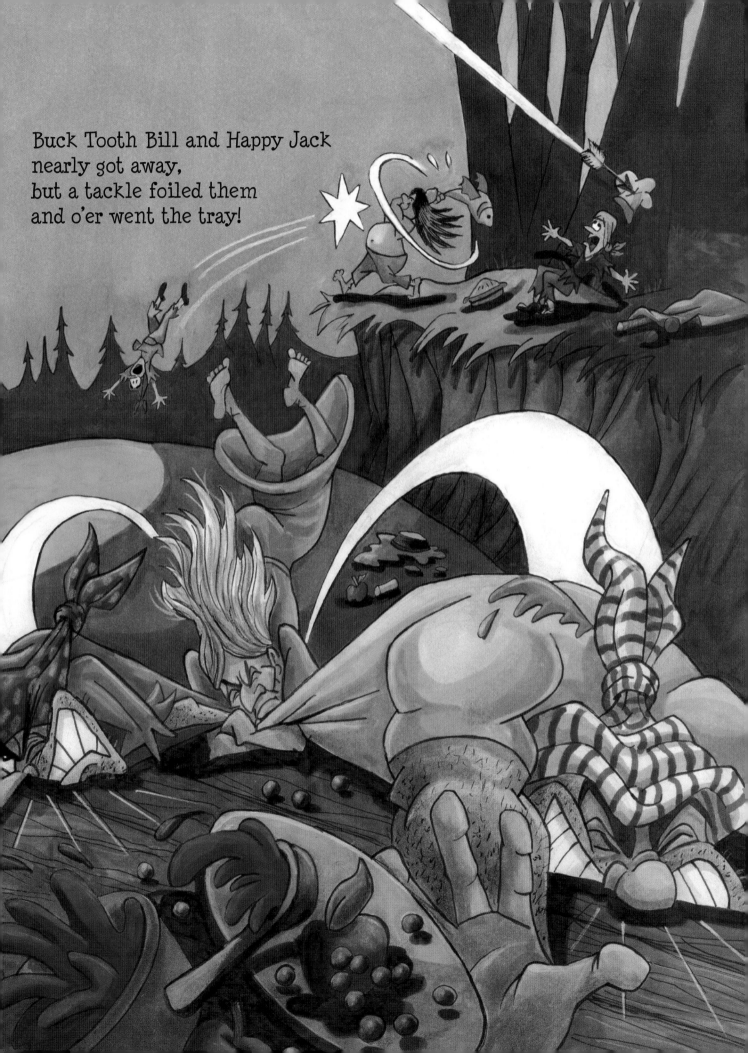

Buck Tooth Bill and Happy Jack
nearly got away,
but a tackle foiled them
and o'er went the tray!

The air was filled with flyin' food,
turnips, corn, and peas.
There was fish a-flyin' high
and turkey in the trees!

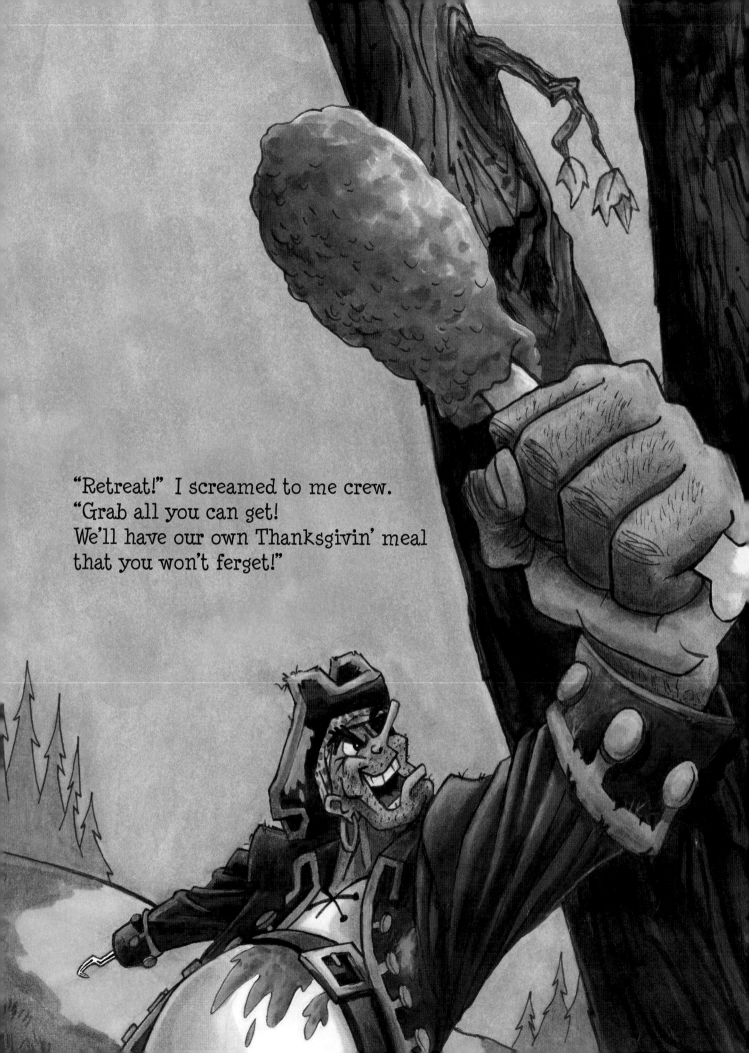

"Retreat!" I screamed to me crew.
"Grab all you can get!
We'll have our own Thanksgivin' meal
that you won't ferget!"

We wuz tired, sore, and hungry
when we hit the dock,
made it to the *Knotty List,*
and sailed from Plymouth Rock.

We wuz the meanest pirates,
sure knew how to steal.
Gathered on the deck with bibs,
ready for our meal.

Thought the crew would be well fed,
with plenty left for me.
But when the spoils were dumped on deck,
there was just a pea!

Author's Note

Thanksgiving is probably the most inclusive of all American holidays. Regardless of race, religion, or economic status, most everyone enjoys a wonderful meal among family and friends, as well as an occasion to reflect on things for which they're thankful. But that's not the only reason it's my favorite time of year—it's also a heck of a lot of fun. Every Thanksgiving meal I ever had growing up was served with a heaping side dish of laughter. In fact, the first Thanksgiving Day, back in 1621, actually lasted *three* days. You can't tell me the Pilgrims and Native Americans weren't having a good time—*no one* hangs out for three days unless there's a lot of great food, friends, laughter, and fun.

I'm not a very good cook, so I can't help you there. But if this book makes you laugh—or just brings a smile to your face—well, for that I'll be thankful. Bon appétit.